MASTER AND MAN

LEO TOLSTOY

MASTER AND MAN

Translated by S. Rapoport
and John C. Kenworthy,
revised by George Gibian

penguin books

PENGUIN BOOKS

Published by the Penguin Group
Penguin Books USA Inc., 375 Hudson Street,
New York, New York 10014, U.S.A.
Penguin Books Ltd, 27 Wrights Lane,
London W8 5TZ, England
Penguin Books Australia Ltd, Ringwood,
Victoria, Australia
Penguin Books Canada Ltd, 10 Alcorn Avenue,
Toronto, Ontario, Canada M4V 3B2
Penguin Books (N.Z.) Ltd, 182–190 Wairau Road,
Auckland 10, New Zealand

Penguin Books Ltd, Registered Offices:
Harmondsworth, Middlesex, England

Published in Penguin Books 1995

ISBN 0 14 60.0089 7

Printed in the United States of America

MASTER AND MAN

I

It happened in the seventies, in winter, on the day after St. Nicholas's day. There was a holiday in the parish, and the village innkeeper and second-guild merchant, Vasily Andreyevich Brekhunov, could not go away, as he had to attend church (he was a church warden), and go receive and entertain friends and acquaintances at home. But at last all the guests were gone, and Vasily Andreyevich began preparations for a drive over to a neighboring landowner to buy from him the forest for which they had been bargaining this long while. He was very anxious to go, so as to forestall the town merchants, who might snatch away this profitable purchase. The youthful landowner only asked ten thousand rubles for the forest, while Vasily Andreyevich offered seven thousand. In reality, seven thousand was but a third of the real worth of the property. Vasily Andreyevich might, perhaps, be able to drive the better bargain, because the forest stood in his district, and by an old-standing agreement between him and the other village-merchants, no one of them competed in another's territory. But Vasily Andreyevich had learned that the timber merchants from the capital town of the province intended to bid for the Goryachkin forest, and he decided to go at once and conclude the bargain. Accordingly, as soon as the feast was over, he took seven hundred rubles of his own from the strongbox, added to them twenty-three hundred belonging to the church, and after carefully counting the whole, he put the money in his pocketbook and made haste to be gone. Nikita, the laborer, the only one of Vasily Andreyevich's men who was not drunk that day, ran to harness the horse. He was not drunk on this occasion because he was a drunkard; since the last day before the fast, when he spent his coat and boots in drink, he had forsworn his debauchery and kept sober for a month. He was not drinking even now, in spite of the temptation arising from the universal absorption of alcohol during the first two days of the holiday.

Nikita was a fifty-year-old muzhik from the neighboring village; an "unreliable" man, as folk called him, "one who lived most of his life with other people" and not at his own home. He was esteemed everywhere for his industry, quickness, and strength, and still more for his kindliness and pleasantness. But he could never live long in one place because about twice a year, or even more often he gave way to drink; and at such times, besides spending all he had, he became turbulent and quarrelsome. Vasily Andreyevich had dismissed him several times, and afterward engaged him again, valuing his honesty and kindness to animals, but chiefly his cheapness. The merchant did not pay Nikita eighty rubles, the worth of such a man, but forty; and even that he paid without regular account, in small installments, and mostly not in cash, but in high-priced goods from his own shop.

Nikita's wife, Martha, a vigorous and once-beautiful woman, carried on the home, with a boy and two girls. She never pressed Nikita to live at home; first, because she had lived for about twenty years with a cooper, a muzhik from another village, who lodged with them; and second, because, although she treated her husband as she pleased when he was sober, she feared him like fire when he was drinking. Once, when drunk at home, Nikita, perhaps to counterbalance his sober humility, broke open his wife's box, took her best clothes, and seizing an ax, cut to shreds all her gala dress and garments. The whole wages that Nikita earned went to his wife, without objection from him. It was in pursuance of this arrangement that Martha, two days before the holiday, came to Vasily Andreyevich, and got from him wheat flour, tea, sugar, with a pint of vodka—about three rubles worth in all—and five rubles in cash; for which she gave thanks as for a great and special favor, when in fact, and at the lowest figure, the merchant owed twenty rubles.

"What agreement did I make with you?" said Vasily Andreyevich to Nikita. "If you want anything, take it; you will work it out. I am not like other folks, with their putting off, and accounts, and fines. We are dealing straightforwardly. You work for me, and I stand by you. What you need, I give it to you."

Talking in this way, the merchant was honestly convinced of his beneficence to Nikita; and he spoke with such assertion that everyone, beginning with Nikita, confirmed him in this conviction.

"I understand, Vasily Andreyevich, I do my best, I try to do as I would for my own father. I understand all right," answered Nikita, understanding very well that he is cheated, but at the same time feeling that it is useless to try to get the accounts cleared up. While there is nowhere else to go, he must stay where he is, and take what he can get.

When Nikita was told by his master to put the horse in, willingly and cheerfully as always, and with a firm and easy stride, he stepped to the cart shed, took down from the nail the heavy, tasseled leather bridle, and jingling the rings of the bit, went to the stable where stood the horse that Vasily Andreyevich had bidden to be harnessed.

"Well, silly, are you tired, tired?" said Nikita, in answer to the soft whinny that greeted him from the stallion, a fairly good dark bay of medium height, with sloping quarters, who stood solitary in his stall. "Quiet, quiet, there's plenty of time! Let me give you a drink first," he went on to the horse, as though speaking to a creature with reason. With the skirt of his coat he swept down the horse's broad, double-ridged back, roughed and dusty as it was; then he put the bridle on the handsome young head, arranged his ears and mane, and led him away to drink. Picking his way out of the dung-strewn stable, the dark bay began to plunge, making play with his hind foot, as though to kick Nikita, who was hurrying him to the well.

"Now, then, now, then, you rogue," said Nikita, knowing Moukhorta was careful that the hind foot went no farther than his fur coat, doing no hurt, and knowing how the horse liked this play.

After the cold water, the horse stood awhile, breathing, and moving his wet, strong lips, from which transparent drops fell into the trough; then he sniffed.

"If you want no more, you needn't take it. Well, let it be at that; but don't ask again for more," said Nikita, quite seriously emphasizing to Moukhorta the consequences of his behavior. Then he briskly led him back to the shed, pulling the rein on the young horse, who lashed out all the way along the yard.

No other men were about, except a stranger to the place, the husband of the cook, who had come for a holiday.

"Go and ask, there's a good fellow, which sleigh is wanted, the wide one or the little one," said Nikita to him.

The cook's husband went away, and soon returned with the answer, that the small one was ordered. By this time, Nikita had harnessed the horse, fixed the brass-studded saddle, and carrying in one hand the light-painted yoke, with the other hand he led the horse toward the two sleighs that stood under the shed.

"All right, let us have the small one," said he, backing the intelligent horse (which all the time pretended to bite at him) into the shafts; and with the help of the cook's husband, he began to harness.

When all was nearly ready, and only the reins needed fixing, Nikita sent the cook's husband to the shed for straw, and to the storehouse for the rug.

"That's nice. Don't, don't don't bristle up!" said Nikita, squeezing into the sleigh the freshly thrashed oat straw that the cook's husband had brought. "Now give me the sacking, while we spread it out, and put the rug over it. That's all right, just the thing, comfortable to sit on," said he, doing that which he was talking about, and making the rug tight over the straw all around.

"Thanks, my dear fellow," said Nikita to the cook's husband. "When two work, it's done quicker." Then, disentangling the leather reins, the ends of which were brought together and tied on a ring, he took the driver's seat on the sleigh and shook up the good horse, who stirred himself, eager to make across the frozen refuse that littered the yard, toward the gate.

"Uncle Mikit, eh, Uncle!" came a shout behind him from a seven-year-old boy in black fur cloak, new white felt boots, and warm cap, who slammed the door as he hurried from the entrance hall toward the yard. "Put me in!" he asked, in a shrill voice, buttoning his cloak as he ran.

"All right, come, my dove," said Nikita; and stopping the sleigh, he put in the master's son, full of joy, and drove out into the road.

It was three o'clock, and cold (about ten degrees of frost), gloomy, and windy. In the yard it seemed quiet, but in the street a strong breeze blew. The snow showered down from the roof of the barn close by and, at the corner by the baths, flew whirling around. Nikita had scarcely driven out and turned around by the front door when Vasily Andreyevich, too, with a cigarette in his mouth, wearing a sheepskin overcoat tightly fastened by a girdle placed low, came out from the entrance hall. He strode down the trampled snow of the steps, which creaked under his boots, and stopped to turn in the corners of his overcoat collar on both sides of his ruddy face (clean-shaven, except for a mustache), so as to keep the fur clear from the moisture of his breath.

"See there! What a manager! Here he is!" said he, smiling and showing his white teeth, on catching sight of his little son on the sleigh. Vasily Andreyevich was excited by the wine he had taken with his guests, and was therefore more than usually pleased with everything that belonged to him, or that was of his doing. His wife, a pale and meager woman, about to become a mother, stood behind him in the entrance hall, with a woolen plaid so wrapped about her head and shoulders that only her eyes could be seen.

"Would it not be better to take Nikita with you?" she asked, timidly, stepping out from the door. Vasily Andreyevich answered nothing, but spat. "You have money with you," the wife continued, in the same plaintive voice. "What if the weather gets worse. Be careful, for God's sake."

"Do you think I don't know the road, that I need a

8

guide?" retorted Vasily Andreyevich, with that affected compression of the lips that he used when speaking among dealers in the market, as though he valued his own speech.

"Really, do take him, I ask you, for God's sake!" repeated his wife, folding her plaid closer.

"Just listen! She sticks to it like a leaf in the bath! Why, where must I take him to?"

"Well, Vasily Andreyevich, I'm ready," said Nikita cheerfully. "If I'm away, there are only the horses to be fed," he added, turning to his mistress.

"I'll look after that, Nikitushka; I'll tell Simon," answered the mistress.

"Shall I come, Vasily Andreyevich?" asked Nikita, waiting.

"It seems we must consider the old woman. But if you come, go and put on something warmer," said Vasily Andreyevich, smiling once more, and winking at Nikita's fur coat, which was very old, torn under the arms and down the back, and soiled and crease-worn around the skirts.

"Hey, friend, come and hold the horse awhile!" shouted Nikita to the cook's husband in the yard.

"I'll hold him myself," said the little boy, taking his cold red hands out of his pockets and seizing the cold leather reins.

"Only don't be too long putting your best coat on! Be quick!" shouted Vasily Andreyevich jestingly to Nikita.

"In a breath, good master Vasily Andreyevich!" said Nikita, and he ran down the yard to the laborers' quarters.

"Now, Arinushka, give me my overcoat off the oven, I have to go with the master!" said Nikita, hastening into the room and taking his girdle down from the nail.

The cook, who had just finished her after-dinner nap, and was about to get ready the samovar for her husband, turned to Nikita merrily, and catching his haste, moved about quickly, took the worn-out woolen overcoat off the oven where it was drying, and shook and rubbed it.

"How comfortable you must be, with your husband here," said Nikita to the cook, always, as part of his good-natured politeness, ready to say something to anyone whom he came across. Then putting around himself the narrow and worn girdle, he drew in his breath and tightened it about his spare body.

"There," he said, afterward, addressing himself not to the cook but to the girdle, while tucking the ends under his belt. "This way you won't jump out." Then working his shoulders up and down to get his arms loose, he put on the overcoat, again stretching his back to free his arms; and that done, he took his mittens from the shelf. "Now we're all right."

"You ought to change your boots," said the cook, "those boots are very bad."

Nikita stopped, as if remembering something.

"Yes, I ought. . . . But it will be all right; it's not far." And he ran out into the yard.

"Won't you be cold, Nikitushka?" said his mistress, as he came up to the sleigh.

"Why should I be cold? It is quite warm," answered Nikita, arranging the straw in the forepart of the sleigh, so as to bring it over the feet, and stowing under it the whip that a good horse would not need.

Vasily Andreyevich was already in the sleigh, almost filling up the whole of the curved back with the bulk of his body wrapped in two great fur coats; and taking up the reins, he started at once. Nikita jumped in, seating himself in front to the left and hanging one leg over the side.

II

The good stallion sped the sleigh along at a brisk pace over the trodden and frozen road, the runners creaking faintly as they went.

"Look at him there, hanging on! Give me the whip, Nikita," shouted Vasily Andreyevich, evidently enjoying the sight of his boy holding to the sleigh runners behind. I'll give it to you! Run to your mother, you young dog!"

The boy jumped off. The dark bay began to amble, and then, getting his breath, broke into a trot.

Kresty, the village where the home of Vasily Andreyevich stood, consisted of six houses. Scarcely had they passed the blacksmith's house when they suddenly felt the wind to be stronger than they had thought. The road was no longer visible. The tracks of the sleigh as they were left behind were instantly covered with snow, and the road was only to be distinguished by its rise above the land on either side. The snow swept over the plain like thick smoke, and the horizon disappeared. The Telyatin forest, always particularly visible, loomed dimly through the driving snow dust. The wind came from the left hand, persistently blowing aside the mane on Moukhorta's lofty neck, turning away even his knotted tail, and pressing the deep collar of Nikita's overcoat (he sat on the windward side) against his face and nose.

"There is no chance of his showing speed with this snow," said Vasily Andreyevich, proud of his horse. "I once went to Pashutino with him, and we got there in half an hour."

"What?"

"Pashutino, I said, and he did it in half an hour."

"A good horse that, no question," said Nikita.

They became silent. But Vasily Andreyevich wanted to talk.

"Now I think of it, did you tell your good woman not to give any drink to the cooper?" asked the merchant, who was wholly of opinion that Nikita must feel flattered, talking with such an important and sensible man as himself. He was so pleased with this, his own jest, that it never entered his head that the subject might be unpleasant to Nikita.

Again the man failed to catch his master's words, the voice being carried away by the wind.

Vasily Andreyevich, in his clear and loud voice, repeated the jest about the cooper.

"God help them, master, I don't think about the matter. I only watch that she does no harm to the boy; if she does—then God help her!"

"That is right," said Vasily Andreyevich. "Well, are you going to buy a horse in the spring?" Thus he began a new topic of conversation.

"I must buy one," answered Nikita, turning aside the collar of his coat and leaning toward his master. The conversation had become interesting to him, and he did not wish to lose a word.

"My lad is grown up, and it is time he plowed for himself and gave up hiring out," said he.

"Well, then, take that horse with the thin loins; the price will not be high," shouted Vasily Andreyevich, eagerly entering into his favorite business of horse dealing, to which he gave all his powers.

"You had better give me fifteen rubles, and I'll buy in the market," said Nikita, who knew that at the highest price, the horse with the thin loins that his master wanted to sell to him was not worth more than seven rubles, but would cost him, at his master's hands, twenty-five; and that meant half a year's wages gone.

"The horse is a good one. I treat you as I would myself. Honestly. Brekhunov injures no man. Let me stand the loss, and me only. Honestly," he shouted in the voice that he used in cheating his customers, "a genuine horse."

"As you think," said Nikita, sighing, sure that it was useless to listen further; and he again drew the collar over his ear and face.

They drove in silence for about half an hour. The wind cut sharply into Nikita's side and arm, where his coat was torn. He huddled himself up and breathed in his coat collar, which covered his mouth, and breathing this way seemed to make him warmer.

"What do you think, shall we go through Karamyshevo, or keep the straight road?" said Vasily Andreyevich.

The road through Karamyshevo was more frequented, and staked on both sides, but it was longer. The straight road was nearer, but it was little used, and the stakes, now snow-covered, marked it out but badly.

Nikita thought awhile.

"Through Karamyshevo is farther, but it is better going," he said.

"But straight on, we have only to be careful in passing the little valley, and then the way is fairly good," said Vasily Andreyevich, who favored the direct road.

"As you say," replied Nikita.

So the merchant went his own way. After driving about half a verst, passing a waymark, a long branch of oak, which shook in the wind and on which a dry leaf hung here and there, he turned to the left.

Upon turning, the wind blew almost directly against them, and the snow showered from on high. Vasily Andreyevich stirred up the horse and inflated his cheeks, blowing his breath upon his mustache. Nikita dozed.

They drove thus silently for about ten minutes. Then the merchant began to say something.

"What?" asked Nikita, opening his eyes.

Vasily Andreyevich did not answer, but bent himself about, looking behind them, and then ahead of the horse. The sweat had curled the animal's coat on the groin and neck, and he was going at a walk.

"I say, what's the matter?" repeated Nikita.

"What is the matter?" mocked Vasily Andreyevich, irritated. "I see no waymarks. We must be off the road."

"Well, pull up, then, and I will find the road," said Nikita, and lightly jumping down, he drew out the whip from the straw and struck out to the left from his own side of the sleigh.

The snow was not deep that season, but in places it was up to one's knee, and Nikita got it into his boots. He walked about, feeling with his feet and the whip, but could nowhere find the road.

"Well?" said the merchant when Nikita returned to the sleigh.

"There is no road on this side. I must try the other."

"What is that dark thing in front? Go and see," said Vasily Andreyevich.

Nikita walked ahead, got near the dark patch, and found it was black earth that the wind had strewn over the snow from some fields of winter wheat. After searching to the right also, he returned to the sleigh, shook the snow off himself, cleared his boots, and took his seat.

"We must go to the right," he said decidedly. "The wind was on our left before, now it is straight ahead. To the right," he repeated, with the same decision.

Vasily Andreyevich turned accordingly. But yet no road was found. He drove on for some time. The wind kept up, and the snow still fell.

"We seem to be astray altogether, Vasily Andreyevich," said Nikita suddenly, and as pleasantly as possible. "What is that?" he said, pointing to some black potato leaves that thrust themselves through the snow.

Vasily Andreyevich stopped the horse, which by this time was in heavy perspiration and stood with its deep sides heaving. "What can it mean?" asked he.

"It means that we are on the Zakharian lands. Why, we are ever so far astray!"

"Bosh!" remarked Vasily Andreyevich, who now spoke quite otherwise than when at home, in an unconstrained and vulgar tone.

"I am telling you no lie; it is true," said Nikita. "You can feel that the sleigh is moving over a potato field, and there are the heaps of old leaves. It is the Zakharian factory land."

"What a long way we are off!" said the other. "What are we to do?"

"Go straight ahead, that's all. We shall reach someplace," said Nikita. "If we do not get to Zakharovka, we shall come out at the owner's farm."

Vasily Andreyevich assented and let the horse go as Nikita had said. They drove in this way for a long while. At times they passed winter wheat fields, where the wind had turned up and blown loose soil over the snow-covered dikes and the snowdrifts. Sometimes they passed a stubble field, sometimes a cornfield, where they could see the upstanding wormwood and straw beaten by the wind; sometimes they saw on all sides deep white snow, with nothing above it. The snow whirled down from on high, and up from below. Now they seemed to be going downhill, and now uphill; then they seemed as though standing still, while the snowfield ran past them. Both were silent. The horse was evidently tiring; his coat grew crisp and white with frost, and he no better than walked. Suddenly he stumbled in some ditch or watercourse and went down. Vasily Andreyevich wanted to halt, but Nikita opposed him.

"Why should we stop? We have gone astray, and we must find our road. Hey, old fellow, hey," he shouted in an encouraging voice to the horse; and he jumped from the sleigh, sinking into the ditch. The horse dashed forward and quickly landed upon a frozen heap. Obviously it was a made ditch.

"Where are we, then?" said Vasily Andreyevich.

"We shall see," answered Nikita. "Go ahead, we shall get to somewhere."

"Is not that the Goryachkin forest?" asked the merchant, pointing out a dark mass that showed across the snow in front of them.

"When we get nearer, we shall see what forest it is," said Nikita.

He noticed that from the side of the dark mass long dry willow leaves were fluttering toward them; and he knew thereby that it was no forest, but houses; yet he chose not to say so. And in fact they had scarcely gone twenty-five yards when they distinctly made out the trees and heard a new and melancholy sound. Nikita was right; they had come upon not a forest but a row of tall willow trees, whereon a few scattered leaves still shivered. The willows were evidently ranged along the ditch and around a barn. Coming up to the trees, through which the wind moaned and sighed, the horse suddenly planted his fore-feet above the height of the sleigh, then drew up his hind legs after him, and they were out of the snow and on the road.

"Here we are," said Nikita, "but we don't know where."

The horse went right away along the snow-covered road, and they had not gone many yards when they saw a fence around a barn, from which the snow was flying in the wind. Passing the barn the road turned in the direction of the wind and brought them upon a snowdrift. But ahead of them was a passage between two houses; the drift was merely blown across the road, and must be crossed. Indeed, after passing the drift, they found a village street. In front of the end house of the village, the wind was shaking desperately the frozen linen that hung there: shirts, one red, one white, some leg cloths, and a skirt. The white shirt especially shook frantically, tugging at the sleeves.

"Look there, either a lazy woman, or a dead one, left her linen out over the holiday," said Nikita, seeing the fluttering shirts.

III

At the beginning of the street the wind was still felt and the road was snow-covered. But well within the village there was shelter, more warmth, and life. At one house a dog barked; at another, a woman, with her husband's coat over her head, came running from within and stopped at the door to see who was driving past. In the middle of the village could be heard the sound of girls singing. Here the wind, the snow, the frost, seemed subdued.

"Why, this is Grishkino," said Vasily Andreyevich.

"It is," said Nikita.

Grishkino it was. It turned out they had strayed eight versts to the left, out of their proper direction; still, they had gotten somewhat nearer to their destination. From Grishkino to Goryachkino was about five versts more.

In the middle of the village they almost ran into a tall man walking in the center of the road.

"Who is driving?" said this man, and he held the horse. Then, recognizing Vasily Andreyevich, he took hold of the shaft and leaped up to the sleigh, where he sat himself on the driver's seat.

It was the muzhik Isai, well-known to the merchant, and known through the district as a first-rate horsethief.

"Ah, Vasily Andreyevich, where is God sending you?" said Isai, from whom Nikita caught the smell of vodka.

"We are going to Goryachkino."

"You've come a long way around! You had better have gone through Malakhovo."

"Yes, but we got astray," said Vasily Andreyevich, pulling up.

"A good horse," said Isai, examining him and dexterously tightening the loosened knot in his tail. "Are you going to stay the night here?"

"No, friend, we must go on."

"Your business must be pressing. And who is that? Ah, Nikita Stepanovich!"

"Who else?" answered Nikita. "Look here, good friend, can you tell us how not to miss the road again?"

"How can you possibly miss it? Just turn back straight along the street, and then, outside the houses, keep straight ahead. Don't go to the left until you reach the high road, then turn to the left."

"And which turning do we take out of the high road? The summer or the winter road?" asked Nikita.

"The winter road. As soon as you get clear of the village there are some bushes, and opposite them is a waymark, an oaken one, all branches. There is the road."

Vasily Andreyevich turned the horse back and drove through the village.

"You had better stay the night," Isai shouted after them. But the merchant did not answer; five versts of smooth road, two versts of it through the forest, was easy enough to drive over, especially as the wind seemed quieter and the snow seemed to have ceased.

After passing along the street, darkened and trodden with fresh horse tracks, and after passing the house where the linen was hung out (a sleeve of the white shirt was by this time torn off, and the garment hung by one frozen sleeve), they came to the weirdly moaning and sighing willows, and then were again in the open country. Not only was the snowstorm still raging, but it seemed to have gained strength. The whole road was under snow, and only the stakes, the waymarks, proved that they were keeping right. But even these signs of the road were difficult to make out, for the wind blew right in their faces.

Vasily Andreyevich screwed up his eyes and bent his head, examining the marks; but for the most part he left the horse alone, trusting to his sagacity. And, in fact, the creature went correctly, turning now to the left, now to the right, along the windings of the road which he sensed under his feet. So that in spite of the thickening snow and strengthening wind, the waymarks were still to be seen, now on the left, now on the right.

They had driven thus for ten minutes when suddenly, straight in front of their horse, a black object sprang up, moving through the snow. Moukhorta had caught up to a sleigh containing other travelers, and he struck his forefeet against it.

"Drive around! Go ahead!" cried these others.

Vasily Andreyevich shaped to go around them. In the sleigh were four peasants, three men and a woman, evidently returning from a feast. One of the men whipped the quarters of their poor horse with a switch, while two of them, waving their arms from the fore part of the sleigh, shouted out something. The woman, muffled up and covered with snow, sat quiet and rigid at the back.

"Who are you?" asked Vasily Andreyevich.

"A-a-a!" was all that could be heard.

"I say, who are you?"

"A-a-a!" shouted one of the peasants with all his strength; but nevertheless it was impossible to make out the name.

"Go on! Don't give up!"

"You have been enjoying yourselves."

"Get on! Get on! Up, Semka! Step out! Up, up!"

The sleighs struck together, almost locked their sides, then fell apart, and the peasants' sleigh began to drop behind. The shaggy, snow-covered, big-bellied pony, obviously distressed, was making his last efforts with his short legs to struggle along through the deep snow, which he trod down with labor. For a moment, with distended nostrils and ears set back in distress, he kept his muzzle, which was that of a young horse, near Nikita's shoulder; then he began to fall still farther behind.

"See what drink does," said Nikita. "They have tired that horse to death. What heathens!"

For a few minutes the pantings of the tired-out horse could be heard, with the drunken shouts of the peasants. Then the pantings become inaudible, and the shouts, also. Again all was silent, except for the whistling wind and the occasional scrape of the sleigh runners upon a bare spot of road.

This encounter livened up and encouraged Vasily Andreyevich, who drove more boldly, not examining the waymarks, and again trusting to his horse.

Nikita had nothing to occupy him, and dozed. Suddenly the horse stopped, and Nikita was jerked forward, knocking his nose against the front.

"It seems we are going wrong again," said Vasily Andreyevich.

"What is the matter?"

"The waymarks are not to be seen. We must be out of the road."

"Well, if so, let us look for the road," said Nikita laconically, and he got out again to explore the snow. He walked for a long time, now out of sight, now reappearing, then disappearing; at last he returned.

"There is no road here; it may be farther on," said he, sitting down in the sleigh.

It began to grow dark. The storm neither increased nor diminished.

"I should like to meet those peasants again," said Vasily Andreyevich.

"Yes, but they won't pass near us; we must be a good distance off the road. Maybe they are astray, too," said Nikita.

"Where shall we make for, then?"

"Leave the horse to himself. He will find his way. Give me the reins."

The merchant handed over the reins, the more willingly that his hands, in spite of his warm gloves, felt the frost.

Nikita took the reins and held them lightly, trying to

give no pressure; he was glad to prove the good sense of his favorite. The intelligent horse, turning one ear and then the other, first in this, then in that direction, presently began to wheel around.

"He only stops short of speaking," said Nikita. "Look how he manages it! Go on, go on, that's good."

The wind was now at their backs; they were warmer.

"Is he not wise?" continued Nikita, delighted with his horse. "A Kirghiz beast is strong, but stupid. But this one—look what he is after with his ears. There is no need of a telegraph wire; he can feel through a mile."

Hardly half an hour had gone when a forest, or a village, or something loomed up in front; and to their right, the waymarks again showed. Evidently they were upon the road again.

"We are back at Grishkino, are we not?" exclaimed Nikita suddenly.

Indeed, on the left hand rose the same barn, with the snow flying from it; and farther on was the same line with the frozen shirts and drawers, so fiercely shaken by the wind.

Again they drove through the street, again felt the quiet and shelter, again saw the road with the horse tracks, heard voices, songs, the barking of a dog. It was now so dark that a few windows were lighted.

Halfway down the street, Vasily Andreyevich turned around the horse toward a large house and stopped at the yard gate.

"Call out Taras," he ordered Nikita.

Nikita went up to the snow-dimmed window, in the light from which glittered the flitting flakes, and knocked with the handle of the whip.

"Who is there?" a voice answered to his knock.

"The Brekhunovs, from Kresty, my good man," answered Nikita. "Come out for a minute."

Someone moved from the window, and in about two minutes the door in the entrance hall was heard to open, the latch of the front door clicked, and holding the door against the wind, there peeped out an old, white-bearded man, who wore a high cap and a fur coat over a white holiday shirt. Behind him was a young fellow in a red shirt and leather boots.

"Glad to see you," said the old man.

"We have lost our road, friend," said Vasily Andreyevich. "We set out for Goryachkino and found ourselves here. Then we went on, but lost the road again."

"I see; what a wandering!" answered the old man. "Petrushka, come, open the gates," he said to the young man in the red shirt.

"Of course I will," said the young fellow cheerfully as he ran off through the entrance hall.

"We are not stopping for the night, friend," said Vasily Andreyevich.

"Where can you go in darkness? You had better stop."

"Should be very glad to, but I must go on."

"Well, then, at least warm yourself a little; the samovar is just ready," said the old man.

"Warm ourselves? We can do that," said Vasily Andreyevich. "It cannot get darker, and when the moon is up, it will be still lighter. Come, Nikita, let us go in and warm up a bit."

"I don't object; yes, let us warm ourselves," said Nikita, who was very cold, and whose one desire was to warm his benumbed limbs over the oven.

Vasily Andreyevich went with the old man into the house. Nikita drove through the gate that Petrushka opened, and by the latter's advice, stood the horse under a shed, the floor of which was strewn with stable litter. The high bow over the horse caught the roof beam, and the hens and a cock perched up there began to cackle and scratch on the wood. Some startled sheep, pattering their feet on the frozen floor, huddled themselves out of the way. A dog, evidently a young one, yelped desperately in fright and barked fiercely at the stranger.

Nikita held conversation with them all. He begged pardon from the fowls, and calmed them with assurances that he would give them no more trouble; he reproved the sheep for being needlessly frightened; and while fastening up the horse, he kept on exhorting the little dog.

"That will do," said he, shaking the snow from himself. "Hear how he is barking!" added he, for the dog's benefit. "That's quite enough for you, quite enough, stupid! That will do! Why do you bother yourself? There are no thieves or strangers about."

"It is like the tale of the Three Domestic Counselors," said the young man, thrusting the sleigh under the shed with his strong arm.

"What counselors?"

"The tale is in P'uls'n. A thief sneaks up to a house; the dog barks—that means 'Don't idle, take care'; the cock crows—that means 'Get up'; the cat washes itself— that means 'A welcome guest is coming, be ready for him,'" said the young man, with a broad smile.

Petrushka could read and write, and knew almost by heart the only book he possessed, which was Paulsen's primer; and he liked, especially when, as now, he had a little too much to drink, to quote from the book some saying that seemed appropriate to the occasion.

"Quite true," said Nikita.

"I suppose you are cold, uncle," said Petrushka.

"Yes, something that way," said Nikita. They both crossed the yard and entered the house.

IV

The house at which Vasily Andreyevich had drawn up
was one of the richest in the village. The family had five
fields, and besides these, hired others outside. Their be-
longings included six horses, three cows, two heifers, and
a score of sheep. In the house lived twenty-two souls; four
married sons, six grandchildren (of whom one, Petrushka,
was married), two great-grandchildren, three orphans,
and four daughters-in-law with their children. It was one
of the few families that maintain their unity; yet even here
was beginning that indefinable interior discord—as usual,
among the women—that must soon bring about separa-
tion. Two sons were water carriers in Moscow; one was in
the army. At present, those at home were the old man, his
wife, one son who was head of the house, another son
who came from Moscow on a holiday, and all the women
and children. Besides the family there was a guest, a
neighbor, who was the elder of the village.

In the house there hung over the table a shaded lamp,
which threw a bright light down upon the tea service, a

bottle of vodka, and some eatables, and upon the brick wall of the corner where hung the holy images with pictures on each side of them. At the head of the table sat Vasily Andreyevich in his black fur coat, sucking his frozen mustache and scrutinizing the people and the room with his eyes of a hawk. Beside him at the table sat the white-bearded bald old father of the house, in a white homespun shirt; by him, wearing a thin cotton shirt, sat a son with sturdy back and shoulders, the one who was holiday-making from Moscow; then the other son, the strapping eldest brother who acted as head of the house; then the village elder, a lean and red-haired muzhik.

The muzhiks, having drunk and eaten, prepared to take tea; the samovar already boiled, standing on the floor near the oven. The children were in evidence about the oven and the sleeping shelves. On the bench along the wall sat a woman with a cradle beside her. The aged mother of the house, whose face was wrinkled all over, even to the lips, waited on Vasily Andreyevich. As Nikita entered the room, she filled up a coarse glass with vodka and handed it to Vasily Andreyevich.

"No harm done, Vasily Andreyevich, but you must drink our good health," said the old man.

The sight and smell of vodka, especially in his cold and tired condition, greatly disturbed Nikita's mind. He became gloomy, and after shaking the snow from his coat and hat, stood before the holy images; without noticing the others, he made the sign of the cross thrice, and bowed to the images; then, turning to the old man, he bowed to him first, afterward to all who sat at the table, and again to the women beside the oven, saying, "Good fortune to your feast." Without looking at the table, he began to take off his overcoat.

"Why, you are all over frost, uncle," said the eldest brother, looking at the rime on Nikita's face, eyes, and beard.

Nikita got his coat off, shook it, hung it near the oven, and came to the table. They offered him vodka also. There was a moment's bitter struggle; he wavered on the point of taking the glass and pouring the fragrant, transparent liquid into his mouth. But he looked at Vasily Andreyevich, remembered his vow, remembered the lost boots, the cooper, his son for whom he had promised to buy a horse when the spring came; he sighed, and refused.

"I don't drink, thank you humbly," he said gloomily, and sat down on the bench near the second window.

"Why not?" asked the eldest brother.

"I don't drink, that's all," said Nikita, not daring to raise his eyes, and looking at the thawing icicles in his beard and mustache.

"It is not good for him," said Vasily Andreyevich, munching a biscuit after emptying his glass.

"Then have some tea," said the kindly old woman. "I daresay you are quite benumbed, good soul. What a while you women are with the samovar."

"It is ready," answered the youngest, and wiping around the samovar with an apron, she bore it heavily to the table and set it down with a thud.

Meanwhile, Vasily Andreyevich told how they had gone astray and worked their way back twice to the same village, what mistakes they had made, and how they had met the drunken peasants. Their hosts expressed surprise, showed why and where they had missed the road, told them the names of the revelers they had met, and made plain how they ought to go.

"From here to Molchanovka, a child might go; the only thing is to make sure where to turn out of the high road, just beside the bushes. But yet you did not get there," said the village elder.

"You ought to stop here. The women will make up a bed," said the old woman persuasively.

"You would make a better start in the morning; much pleasanter, that," said the old man, affirming what his wife had said.

"Impossible, friend! Business!" said Vasily Andreyevich.

"If you let an hour go, you may not be able to make it up in a year," added he, remembering the forest and the dealers who were likely to compete with him. "By all means, let us stretch out," he said, turning to Nikita.

"We may lose ourselves again," said Nikita moodily. He was gloomy because of the intense longing he felt for the vodka; and the tea, the only thing that could quench that longing, had not yet been offered to him.

"We have only to reach the turning, and there is no more danger of losing the road, as it goes straight through the forest," said Vasily Andreyevich.

"Just as you say, Vasily Andreyevich; if you want to go, let us go," said Nikita, taking the glass of tea offered to him.

"Well, let us drink up our tea, and then march!"

Nikita said nothing, but shook his head, and carefully pouring the tea into the saucer, began to warm his hands over the steam. Then, taking a small bite of sugar in his mouth, he turned to their hosts, said "Your health," and drank down the warming liquid.

"Could anyone come with us to the turning?" asked Vasily Andreyevich.

"Why not? Certainly," said the eldest son. "Petrushka will put in the horse and go with you as far as the turning."

"Then put in your horse, and I shall be in your debt."

"My dear man," said the kindly old woman, "we are right glad to do it."

"Petrushka, go and put in the mare," said the eldest son.

"All right," said Petrushka, with his broad smile; and taking his cap from the nail, he hurried away to harness the horse.

While the harnessing was in progress, the talk turned back to the point where it stood when Vasily Andreyevich arrived. The old man had complained to the village elder about the conduct of his third son, who had sent him no present this holiday time, though he had sent a French shawl to his wife.

"These young folk are getting worse and worse," said the old man.

"Very much worse!" said the village elder. "They are unmanageable. They know too much. There's Demochkin, now, who broke his father's arm. It all comes from too much learning."

Nikita listened, watched the faces, seeming as though he, too, would like to have a share in the conversation, were he not so busy with his tea; as it was, he only nodded his head approvingly. He emptied glass after glass, growing warmer and more and more comfortable. The

37

talk kept on in the one strain, all about the harm that comes from family division; clearly, no theoretical discussion, but concerned with a rupture in this very house, arising through the second son, who sat there in his place, morosely silent. The question was a painful one, and absorbed the whole family; but in politeness they refrained from discussing their private affairs before strangers. At last, however, the old man could endure no longer. In a tearful voice, he began to say that there should be no breakup of the family while he lived, that the house had much to thank God for, but if they fell apart—they must become beggars.

"Just like the Matvayeffs," said the village elder. "There was plenty among them all, but when they broke up the family, there was nothing for any of them."

"That's just what you want to do," said the old man to his son.

The son answered nothing, and there was a painful pause. Petrushka broke the silence, having by this time harnessed the horse and returned to the room, where he had been standing for a few minutes, smiling all the time.

"There is a tale in P'uls'n, just like this," said he. "A father gave his sons a besom to break. They could not break it while it was bound together, but they broke it easily by taking every switch by itself. That's the way here," he said, with his broad smile. "All's ready!" he added.

"Well, if we're ready, let us start," said Vasily Andreyevich. "As to this quarrel, don't you give in, grandfather. You got everything together, and you are the master. Apply to the magistrate; he will show you how to keep your authority."

"And he gives himself such airs, such airs," the old man continued to complain, appealingly. "There is no ordering him! It is as though Satan lived in him."

Meanwhile, Nikita, having drunk his fifth glass of tea, did not stand it upside down, in sign that he had finished, but laid it by his side, hoping they might fill it a sixth time. But as the samovar had run dry, the hostess did not fill up for him again; and then Vasily Andreyevich began to put on his things. There was no help; Nikita, too, rose, put back his nibbled little cake of sugar into the sugar basin, wiped the moisture from his face with the skirt of his coat, and moved to put on his overcoat.

After getting into the garment, he sighed heavily, then, having thanked their hosts and said good-bye, he went out from the warm, bright room and through the dark, cold entrance hall, where the wind creaked the doors and drove the snow in at the chinks, into the dark yard. Petrushka, in his fur coat, stood in the center of the yard with the horse, and smiling as ever, recited a verse from "P'uls'n":

> *The storm covers the heaven with darkness,*
> *Whirling the driven snow,*
> *Now, howling like a wild beast,*
> *Now, crying like a child.*

Nikita nodded appreciatively, and arranged the reins.

The old man, coming out with Vasily Andreyevich, brought a lantern, wishing to show the way; but the wind put it out at once. Even in the enclosed yard, one could see that the storm had risen greatly.

"What weather!" thought Vasily Andreyevich. "I'm afraid we shall not get there. But it must be! Business! And then, I have put our friend to the trouble of harnessing his horse, God helping, we'll get there."

Their aged host also thought it better not to go; but he had offered his arguments already, and they had not been listened to. "Maybe it is old age makes me overcautious; they will get there all right," thought he. "And we can all go to bed at the proper time. It will be less bother."

Petrushka likewise saw danger in going, and felt uneasy; but he would not let anyone see it, and put on a bold front, as though he had not a fear; the lines about "whirling the driven snow" encouraged him, because they were a quite true description of what was going on out in the street. As to Nikita, he had no wish to go at all; but he was long used to following other people's wishes, and to give up his own. Therefore nobody withheld the travelers.

V

Vasily Andreyevich went over to the sleighs, found them with some groping through the darkness, got in, and took the reins.

"Go ahead!" he shouted. Petrushka, kneeling in his sleigh, started the horse. The dark bay, who had before been whinnying, aware of the mare's nearness, now dashed after her, and they drove out into the street. They rode once more through the village, down the same road, past the space where the frozen linen had hung, but hung no longer; past the same barn, now snowed-up almost as high as the roof, from which the snow flew incessantly; past the moaning, whistling, and bending willows. And again they came to where the sea of snow raged from above and below. The wind had such power that, taking the travelers sideways when they were crossing its direction, it heeled the sleigh over so that the horse was pushed aside. Petrushka drove his good mare in front, at an easy trot, giving her an occasional lively shout of encouragement. The dark bay pressed after her.

After driving thus for about ten minutes, Petrushka turned around and called out something. But neither Vasily Andreyevich nor Nikita could hear for the wind, but they guessed that they had reached the turning. In fact, Petrushka had turned to the right; the wind came in their front, and to the right, through the snow, loomed something black. It was the bush beside the turning.

"Well, good-bye to you!"

"Thanks, Petrushka!"

" 'The storm covers the heaven with darkness!' " shouted Petrushka, and disappeared.

"Quite a poet," said Vasily Andreyevich, and shook the reins.

"Yes, a fine young man, a genuine fellow," said Nikita.

They drove on. Nikita sank and pressed his head between his shoulders, so that his short beard covered up his throat. He sat silent, trying to keep the warmth that the tea had given him. Before him he saw the straight lines of the shafts, which to his eyes looked like the ruts of the road; he saw the shifting quarters of the horse, with the knotted tail swayed in the wind; beyond, he saw the high bow between the shafts, and the horse's rocking head and neck, with the floating mane. From time to time he noticed waymarks, and knew that, thus far, they had kept right, and he need not concern himself.

Vasily Andreyevich drove on, trusting to the horse to keep to the road. But Moukhorta, although he had picked himself up a little in the village, went unwillingly, and seemed to shirk from the road, so that Vasily Andreyevich had to press him at times.

"Here is a waymark on the right, here's another, and there's a third," reckoned Vasily Andreyevich, "and here, in front, is the forest," he thought, examining a dark patch ahead. But that which he took for a forest was only a bush. They passed the bush, drove about fifty yards farther, and there was neither the fourth waymark nor the forest.

"We must reach the forest soon," thought Vasily Andreyevich; and buoyed up by the vodka and the tea, he shook the reins. The good, obedient animal responded, and now at an amble, now at an easy trot, made in the direction he was sent, although he knew it was not the way in which he should have been going. Ten minutes went by, but no forest.

"I'm afraid we are lost again!" said Vasily Andreyevich, pulling up.

Nikita silently got out from the sleigh, and holding with his hand the flaps of his coat, which pressed against him or flew from him as he stood and turned in the wind, began to tread the snow, first to one side, then to the other. About three times he went out of sight altogether. At last he returned and took the reins from the hands of Vasily Andreyevich.

"We must go to the right," he said sternly and peremptorily; and he turned the horse.

"Well, if it must be to the right, let us go to the right," said Vasily Andreyevich, passing over the reins and thrusting his hands into his sleeves. "I should be glad to be back at Grishkino, anyway," he said.

Nikita did not answer.

"Now, then, old fellow, stir yourself," he called to the horse; but the latter, in spite of the shake of the reins, went on only slowly. In places the snow was knee-deep, and the sleigh jerked at every movement of the horse.

Nikita took the whip, which hung in front of the sleigh, and struck once. The good creature, unused to the lash, sprang forward at a trot, but soon fell again to a slow amble. Thus they went for five minutes. All was so dark, and so blurred with snow from above and below, that sometimes they could not make out the bow between the shafts. At times it seemed as though the sleigh was standing, and the ground running back. Suddenly the horse stopped, feeling something wrong in front of him. Nikita once more lightly jumped out, throwing down the reins, and went in front to find out what was the matter. But hardly had he taken a pace clear ahead, when his feet slipped and he fell down some steep place.

"Whoa, whoa!" he said to himself, trying to stop his fall, and falling. There was nothing to seize hold of, and he only brought up when his feet plunged into a thick bed of snow that lay in the ravine. The fringe of snow that hung on the edge of the ravine, disturbed by Nikita's fall, showered upon him, and got into his coat collar.

"That's bad treatment!" said Nikita, reproaching the snow and the ravine, as he cleared out his coat collar.

"Mikit, ha, Mikit," shouted Vasily Andreyevich, from above. But Nikita did not answer. He was too much occupied in shaking away the snow, then in looking for the whip, which he lost in rolling down the bank. Having found the whip, he started to climb up the bank, but failed, rolling back every time, so that he was compelled to go along the foot of the bank to find a way up. About ten yards from the place where he fell, he managed to struggle up again, and turn back along the bank toward where the horse should have been. He could not see horse nor sleigh; but by going over in the direction to which the wind was blowing, he heard the voice of Vasily Andreyevich and the whinny of Moukhorta calling him, before he saw them.

"I'm coming. Don't make a noise for nothing," he said.

Only when quite near the sleigh could he make out the horse and Vasily Andreyevich, who stood close by, and looked gigantic.

"Where the devil have you gotten lost? We've got to drive back. We must get back to Grishkino anyway," the master began to rebuke him angrily.

"I should be glad to get there, Vasily Andreyevich, but how are we to do it? Here is a ravine where if we once get in, we shall never come out. I pitched in there in such a way that I could hardly get out."

"Well, surely we can't stay here; we must go somewhere," said Vasily Andreyevich.

Nikita made no answer. He sat down on the sleigh with his back to the wind, took off his boots and emptied them of snow, then, with a little straw that he took from the sleigh, he stopped from the inside a gap in the left boot.

Vasily Andreyevich was silent, as though leaving everything to Nikita alone. Having put on his boots, Nikita drew his feet into the sleigh, took the reins, and turned the horse along the ravine. But they had not driven a hundred paces when the horse stopped again. Another ditch confronted him.

Nikita got out again and began to explore the snow. He was afoot a long while. At last he reappeared on the side opposite to that from which he started.

"Vasily Andreyevich, are you alive?" he called.

"Here! What is the matter?"

"I can't make anything out, it is too dark; except some ditches. We must drive to windward again."

They set off once more; Nikita explored again, stumbling in the snow, or resting on the sleigh; at last, falling down, he was out of breath, and stopped beside the sleigh.

"How now?" asked Vasily Andreyevich.

"Well, I'm quite tired out. And the horse is done up."

"What are we to do?"

"Wait a minute." Nikita moved off again, and soon returned.

"Follow me," he said, going in front of the horse.

Vasily Andreyevich gave orders no more, but implicitly did what Nikita told him.

"Here, this way," shouted Nikita, stepping quickly to the right. Seizing Moukhorta's head, he turned him toward a snowdrift. At first the horse resisted, then dashed forward, hoping to leap the drift, but failed and sank in snow up to the hams.

"Get out!" called Nikita to Vasily Andreyevich, who still sat in the sleigh; and taking hold of a shaft, he began to push the sleigh after the horse.

"It's a hard job, friend," he said to Moukhorta, "but it

can't be helped. Stir yourself! Once more! Ah-oo-oo! Just a little!" he called out. The horse leaped forward, once, twice, but failed to clear himself, and sank again. He pricked his ears and sniffed at the snow, putting his head down to it as if thinking out something.

"Well, friend, this is no good," urged Nikita to Moukhorta. "A-ah, just a little more!" Nikita pulled on the shaft again; Vasily Andreyevich did the same on the opposite side. The horse lifted his head and made a sudden dash.

"A-ah, A-ah, don't be afraid, you won't sink," shouted Nikita. One plunge, a second, a third, and at last the horse was out from the snowdrift and stood still, breathing heavily and shaking himself clear. Nikita wanted to lead him on farther; but Vasily Andreyevich, in his two fur coats, had so lost his breath that he could walk no more, and dropped into the sleigh.

"Let me get my breath a little," he said, unbinding the handkerchief that tied the collar of his coat.

"We are all right here, you might as well lie down," said Nikita. "I'll lead him along"; and with Vasily Andreyevich in the sleigh, he led the horse by the head, about ten paces farther, then up a slight rise, and stopped.

The place where Nikita drew up was not in a hollow, where the snow might gather, but was sheltered from the wind by rising ground. At moments the wind, outside this protection, seemed to become quieter; but these intervals did not last long, and after them the storm, as if to compensate itself, rushed on with tenfold vigor, and tore and whirled the more. Such a gust of wind swept past as Vasily Andreyevich, with recovered breath, got out of the sleigh and went up to Nikita to talk over the situation. They both instinctively bowed themselves, and waited until the stress should be over. Moukhorta laid back his ears and shook himself discontentedly. When the blast had abated a little, Nikita took off his mittens, stuck them in his girdle, and having breathed a little on his hands, began to undo the strap from the bow over the shafts.

"Why are you doing that?" asked Vasily Andreyevich.

"I'm taking out the horse. What else can we do? I'm worn out," said Nikita, as though apologizing.

"But we could drive out to somewhere."

"No, we could not. We should only do harm to the horse. The poor beast is worn out," said Nikita, pointing to the creature, who stood there, awaiting the next move with heavily heaving sides. "We must put up for the night," he repeated, as though they were at their inn. He began to undo the collar straps, and detached the collar.

"But we shall be frozen?" queried Vasily Andreyevich.

"Well, if we are, we cannot help it," said Nikita.

VI

In his two fur coats, Vasily Andreyevich was quite warm, especially after the exertion in the snowdrift. But a cold shiver ran down his back when he learned that they must stay where they were the night long. To calm himself, he sat down in the sleigh and got out his cigarettes and matches.

Meanwhile, Nikita continued to take out the horse. He undid the belly band, took away the reins and collar strap, and laid the bow aside from the shafts, continuing to encourage Moukhorta by speaking to him.

"Now, come out, come out," he said, leading the horse clear of the shafts. "We must tie you here. I'll put a bit of straw for you, and take off your bridle," he went on, doing as he said. "After a bite, you'll feel ever so much better."

But Moukhorta was not calmed by Nikita's words; uneasily he shifted his feet, pressed against the sleigh, turned his back to the wind, and rubbed his head on Nikita's sleeve.

As if not wholly to reject the treat of straw that Nikita put under his nose, Moukhorta just once seized a wisp out of the sleigh, but quickly deciding that there was more important business than to eat straw, he threw it down again, and the wind instantly tore it away and hid it in the snow.

"Now we must make a signal," said Nikita, turning the front of the sleigh against the wind; and having tied the shafts together with a strap, he set them on end in the front of the sleigh. "If the snow covers us, the good folk will see the shafts and dig us up," said Nikita. "That's what old hands advise."

Vasily Andreyevich had meanwhile opened his fur coat, and making a shelter with its folds, he rubbed match after match on the box. But his hands trembled, and the kindled matches were blown out by the wind, one after another, some when just struck, others when he thrust them to the cigarette. At last one match burned fully and lighted up for a moment the fur of his coat, his hand with the gold ring on the bent forefinger, and the snow-sprinkled straw that stuck out from under the sacking. The cigarette took light. Twice he eagerly whiffed the smoke, drew it in, blew it through his mustache, and would have gone on, but the wind tore away the burning tobacco. Even these few whiffs of tobacco smoke cheered up Vasily Andreyevich.

"Well, we will stop here," he said authoritatively.

Looking at the raised shafts, he thought to make a still better signal, and to give Nikita a lesson.

"Wait a minute, and I'll make a flag," he said picking up the handkerchief that he had taken from around his collar and put down in the sleigh. Drawing off his gloves and reaching up, he tied the handkerchief tightly to the strap that held the shafts together. The handkerchief at once began to beat about wildly, now clinging around a shaft, now streaming out, and cracking like a whip.

"That's fine," said Vasily Andreyevich, pleased with his work, and getting into the sleigh. "We should be warmer together, but there's not room for two," he said.

"I can find room," said Nikita, "but the horse must be covered; he's sweating, the good fellow. Excuse me," he added, going to the sleigh and drawing the sacking from under Vasily Andreyevich. This he folded, and after taking off the saddle and breeching, covered the dark bay with it.

"Anyway, it will be a bit warmer, silly," he said, putting the saddle and heavy breeching over the sacking.

"Can you spare the rug? and give me a little straw?" said Nikita, after finishing with the horse.

Taking these from under Vasily Andreyevich, he went behind the sleigh, dug there a hole in the snow, put in the straw, and pulling his hat over his eyes and covering himself with the rug, sat down on the straw, with his back against the bark matting of the back of the sleigh, which kept off the wind and snow.

Vasily Andreyevich, seeing what Nikita was doing, shook his head disapprovingly, in the way he usually did over the signs of peasant folks' ignorance and denseness; and he began to make arrangements for the night.

He smoothed the remaining straw, heaped it more thickly under his side, thrust his hands into his sleeves, and adjusted his head in the corner of the sleigh in front, where he was sheltered from the wind. He did not wish to sleep. He lay down and thought; about one thing only, which was the aim, reason, pleasure, and pride of his life; about the money he had made, and might make, the amount his neighbors had, and the means whereby they gained it and were gaining it; and how he, like them, could gain a great deal more.

"The oak can be sold for sleigh runners. And certainly, the trees for building. And there are a hundred feet of firewood to the acre"—so he estimated the forest, which he had seen in the autumn, and which he was going to buy. "But for all that, I won't pay ten thousand; say eight thousand; and besides, in allowing for the bare spaces, I'll oil the surveyor—a hundred rubles will do it—a hundred and fifty, if necessary, and get him to take about thirteen acres out of the forest. He is sure to sell for eight; three thousand down. Yes, sure; he will weaken at that," he thought, pressing his forearm on the pocketbook beneath. "And how we've gotten astray, God knows! The forest and the keeper's hut should be just by. I should like to hear the dogs, but they never bark when they're wanted, the cursed brutes." He opened his collar a little to look and listen; there was only the dark head of the horse, and his back, on which the sackcloth fluttered; there was only the same whistle of the wind, the flapping and cracking of the handkerchief on the shafts, and the lashing of the snow on the bark matting of the sleigh. He covered himself again. "If one had only known this beforehand, we had better have stayed where we were. But no matter; tomorrow will be time enough. It is only a day later. In this weather, the other fellows won't dare to go." Then he remembered that on the ninth he had to receive the price of some cattle from the butcher. He wanted to do the business himself, for his wife had no experience, and was not competent in such matters. "She never knows what to do," he continued to reflect, remembering how she had failed in her behavior toward the commissary of police when he visited them yesterday at the feast. "Just a woman, of course. What has she ever seen? In my father's and mother's time, what sort of a house had we? Nothing out of the way; a well-to-do countryman's; a barn, and an inn, and that was the whole property. And now what a change I've made, these fifteen years! A general store, two taverns, a flour mill, a stock of grain, two farms rented, a house and warehouse all iron-roofed," he remembered proudly. "Not like in the old people's time! Who is known over the whole place? Brekhunov.

"And why is all this? Because I stick to business, I look after things; not like others, who idle, or waste their time in foolishness. I give up sleep at night. Storm or no storm, I go. And of course, the thing is done. They think money is made easily, by just playing. Not at all; it's work and trouble. They think luck makes men. Look at the Mironovs, who have their millions, now. Why? They worked. Then God gives. If God only grants us health!" And the idea that he, also, might become a millionaire like Mironov, who began with nothing, so excited Vasily Andreyevich that he suddenly felt a need to talk to someone. But there was nobody. If he could only have reached Goryachkino, he might have talked with the landowner, and got around him.

"What a gale! It will snow us in so that we can't get out

56

in the morning," he thought, listening to the sound of the wind, which blew against the front of the sleigh and lashed the snow against the bark matting.

"And I did as Nikita said, all for nothing," he thought. "We ought to have driven on, and gotten to somewhere. We might have gone back to Grishkino and stayed at Taras's. Now we must sit here all night. Well, what was I thinking about? Yes, that God gives to the industrious, and not to the lazy, loafers, and fools. It's time for a smoke, too." He sat up, got his cigarette case, and stretched himself flat on his stomach, to protect the light from the wind with the flaps of his coat; but the wind got in and put out match after match. At least he managed to get a cigarette lit. It began to burn, and the achievement of his object greatly delighted him. Although the wind had more of his cigarette than he himself, nevertheless he got about three puffs, and felt better. He again threw himself back in the sleigh, wrapped himself up, and returned to his recollections and dreams; he fell asleep. But suddenly something pushed and awoke him. Was it the dark bay pulling the straw from under him, or some fancy of his own? At all events he awoke, and his heart began to beat so quickly and strongly that the sleigh seemed to be shaking under him. He opened his eyes. Everything around was the same as before; but it seemed a shade brighter. "The morning," he thought, "it can't be far from morning." But he suddenly remembered that the light was only due to the rising of the moon. He lifted himself, and looked first at the horse. Moukhorta stood with his back to the wind and shivered all over. The sacking, snow-covered and turned up at one corner; the breeching, which had slipped aside; the snowy head and fluttering mane; all was now more clearly visible. Vasily Andreyevich bent over the back of the sleigh and looked behind. Nikita sat in his old position. The rug and his feet were covered with snow. "I'm afraid he will be frozen, his clothes are so bad. I might be held responsible. He is tired out, and has not much resisting power," reflected Vasily Andreyevich; and he thought of taking the sacking from the horse, to put over Nikita; but it was cold to disturb himself, and besides, he did not want the horse frozen. "What was the use of bringing him? It is all her stupidity!" thought Vasily Andreyevich, remembering the unloved wife; and he turned again to his former place in the front of the sleigh. "My uncle once sat in snow all night like this," he reflected, "and no harm came of it. And Sebastian also was dug out," he went on, remembering another case, "but he was dead, stiff like a frozen carcass.

"It would have been all right if we had stopped at

Grishkino." Carefully covering himself, not to waste the warmth of the fur, and so as to protect his neck, knees, and the soles of his feet, he shut his eyes, trying to sleep. But however much he tried, no sleep came; on the contrary, he felt alert and excited. He began again to count his gains and the debts due to him; again he began to boast to himself, and to feel proud of himself and his position; but he was all the while disturbed by a lurking fear, and by the unpleasant reflection that he had not stopped at Grishkino. He changed his attitude several times; he lay down and tried to find a better position, more sheltered from wind and snow, but failed; he rose again and changed his position, crossed his feet, shut his eyes, and lay silent; but either his crossed feet, in their high felt boots, began to ache, or the wind blew in somewhere. Thus lying for a short time, he again began the disagreeable reflection, how comfortably he would have lain in the warm house at Grishkino. Again he rose, changed his position, wrapped himself up, and again lay down.

Once Vasily Andreyevich fancied he heard a distant cock crow. He brightened up and began to listen with all his might; but however he strained his ear, he heard nothing but the sound of the wind whistling against the shafts, and the snow lashing the bark matting of the sleigh.

Nikita had been motionless all the time, not even answering Vasily Andreyevich, who spoke to him twice.

"He doesn't worry; he seems to be asleep," Vasily Andreyevich thought angrily, looking behind the sleigh at the snow-covered Nikita.

Twenty times Vasily Andreyevich thus rose and lay down. It seemed to him this night would never end. "It must be near morning now," he thought once, rising and looking around him. "Let me see my watch. It is cold to unbutton oneself; but if I only knew it was near morning, it would be better. Then we might begin to harness the horse." At the bottom of his mind, Vasily Andreyevich knew that the dawn could be nowhere near; but he began to feel more and more afraid, and he chose both to deceive himself and to find himself out. He began cautiously to undo the hooks of the inside fur coat, then putting his hands in at the bosom, he felt about until he got at the vest. With great trouble, he drew out his silver, flower-enameled watch, and began to examine it. Without a light, he could make out nothing. Again he lay down flat, as when he lit the cigarette, got the matches, and began to strike. This time he was particularly careful, and selecting a match with most phosphorus on, at one attempt lit it. Lighting up the face of the watch, he could not believe his eyes. It was not later than ten minutes past twelve. The whole night was yet before him.

"Oh, what a weary night!" thought Vasily Andreyevich, a cold shiver running down his back; and buttoning up again, he hugged himself close in the corner of the sleigh. Suddenly, through the monotonous wail of the wind, he distinctly heard a new and a living sound. It grew gradually louder and became quite clear, then began to die away. There could be no doubt; it was a wolf. And this wolf's howl was so near that down the wind one could hear how he changed his cry by the movement of his jaws. Vasily Andreyevich turned back his collar and listened attentively. Moukhorta listened likewise, pricking up his ears, and when the wolf had ceased howling, he shifted his feet and sniffed warningly. After this Vasily Andreyevich not only was unable to sleep, but even to keep calm. The more he tried to think of his accounts, of his business, reputation, importance, and property, more and more fear grew upon him; and above all his thoughts, one thought stood out predominantly and penetratingly: the thought of his rashness in not stopping at Grishkino.

"The forest—what do I care about the forest? There is plenty of business without that, thank God! Ah, why did I not stay the night?" said he to himself. "They say people who drink are soon frozen," he thought, "and I have had some drink." Then testing his own sensations, he felt that he began to shiver, not knowing whether from cold or fear. He tried to wrap himself up and to lie down as before; but he could not. He was unable to rest, wanted to rise, to do something to suppress his gathering fears, against which he felt helpless. Again he got his cigarettes and matches; but only three of the latter remained, and these were bad ones. All three rubbed away without lighting.

"To the devil, curse it, to—!" he broke out, himself not knowing why, and he threw away the cigarette, broken. He was about to throw away the matchbox, but stayed his hand, and thrust it in his pocket instead. He was so agitated that he could no longer remain in one place. He got out of the sleigh, and standing with his back to the wind, set his girdle again, tightly and low down.

"What is the use of lying down; it is only waiting for death; much better mount the horse and get away!" The thought suddenly flashed into his mind. "The horse will not stand still with someone on his back. He"—thinking of Nikita—"must die anyway. What sort of a life has he? He does not care much even about his life, but as for me—thank God, I have something to live for!"

Untying the horse from the sleigh, he threw the reins over his neck and tried to mount, but failed. Then he clambered on the sleigh, and tried to mount from that; but the sleigh tilted under his weight, and he failed again. At last, on a third attempt, he backed the horse to the sleigh, and cautiously balancing on the edge, got his body across the horse. Lying thus for a moment, he pushed himself once, twice, and finally threw one leg over and seated himself, supporting his feet on the breeching in place of stirrups. The shaking of the sleigh roused Nikita, and he got up; Vasily Andreyevich thought he was speaking.

"Listen to you, fool? What, must I die in this way, for nothing?" exclaimed Vasily Andreyevich. Tucking under his knees the loose skirts of his fur coat, he turned the horse around and rode away from the sleigh in the direction where he expected to find the forest and the keeper's hut.

VII

Nikita had not stirred since, covered by the rug, he took his seat behind the sleigh. Like all people who live with nature, and endure much, he was patient and could wait for hours, even days, without growing restless or irritated. When his master called to him, he heard, but made no answer, because he did not wish to stir. The thought that he might, and very likely must, die that night came to him at the moment he was taking his seat behind the sleigh. Although he still felt the warmth from the tea he had taken, and from the exercise of struggling through the snowdrift, he knew the warmth would not last long, and that he could not warm himself again by moving about, for he was exhausted and felt as a horse may when it stops and must have food before it can work again. Besides, his foot, the one in the torn boot, was numbed, and already he could not feel the great toe. And the cold began to creep all over his body.

The thought that he would die that night came upon him, seeming not very unpleasant, nor very awful. Not unpleasant, because his life had been no unbroken feast, but rather an incessant round of toil of which he began to weary. And not awful, because, beyond the masters whom he served here, like Vasily Andreyevich, he felt himself dependent upon the Great Master; upon Him who had sent him into this life. And he knew that even after death he must remain in the power of that Master, who would not treat him badly. "Is it a pity to leave what you are practiced in and used to? Well, what's to be done? You must get used to fresh things as well.

"Sins?" he thought, and recollected his drunkenness, the money wasted in drink, his ill treatment of his wife, neglect of church and of the fasts, and all things for which the priest reprimanded him at the confessional. "Of course, these are sins. But then, did I bring them on me myself? Whatever I am, I suppose God made me so. Well, and about these sins? How can one help it?"

So he thought, concerning what might happen to him that night, and having reached his conclusion, he gave himself up to the thoughts and recollections that ran through his mind of themselves. He remembered the visit of his wife, Martha; the drunkenness among the peasants, and his own abstinence from drink; the beginning of their journey; Tarass's house, and the talk about the breakup of the family; his own lad; Moukhorta, with the sacking over him for warmth; and his master, rolling around in the sleigh and making it creak. "He is uneasy," thought Nikita, "most likely because a life like his makes one want not to die; different from people of my kind." And all these recollections and thoughts interwove and jumbled themselves in his brain, until he fell asleep.

When Vasily Andreyevich mounted the horse, he twisted aside the sleigh, and the back of it slid away from behind Nikita, who was struck by one of the runner ends. Nikita awoke, thus compelled to move. Straightening his legs with difficulty, and throwing off the snow that covered them, he got up. Instantly an agony of cold penetrated his whole frame. On making out what was happening, he wanted Vasily Andreyevich to leave him the sacking that lay over the horse, which was no longer needed there, so that he might put it around himself. But Vasily Andreyevich did not wait, and disappeared in the midst of snow. Thus left alone, Nikita considered what he had better do. He felt unable to move off in search of some house; and it was already impossible for him to sit down in the place he had occupied, for it was already covered with snow; and he knew he could not get warm in the sleigh, having nothing to cover him. He felt as cold as though he stood in his shirt; there seemed no warmth at all from his coat and overcoat. For a moment he pondered, then sighed, and keeping the rug over his head, he threw himself into the sleigh, in the place where his master had lain. He huddled himself up into the smallest space, but still got no warmth. Thus he lay for about five minutes, shivering through his whole body; then the shivering ceased, and he began to lose consciousness, little by little. Whether he was dying or falling asleep, he knew not; but he was as ready for the one as for the other. If God should bid him get up again, still alive in the world, to go on with his laborer's life, to care for other men's horses, to carry other men's grain to the mill, to again start drinking and renouncing drink, to continue the money supply to his wife and that same cooper, to watch his lad growing up—well, so be His holy will. Should God bid him arise in another world, where all would be as fresh and bright as this world was in his young childhood, with the caresses of his mother, the games among the children, the fields, forests, skating in winter—arise to a life quite out of the common—then, so be His holy will. And Nikita wholly lost consciousness.

VIII

During this while, Vasily Andreyevich, guiding with his feet and the gathered reins, rode the horse in the direction where he, for some cause, expected to find the forest and the forester's hut. The snow blinded him, and the wind, it seemed, was bent on staying him; but with head bent forward, and continually pulling up his fur coat between him and the cold, nail-studded pad on which he could not settle himself, he urged on the horse. The dark bay, though with difficulty, obediently ambled on in the direction to which he was turned.

For some minutes he rode on—as it seemed to him, in a straight line—seeing nothing but the horse's head and the white waste, and hearing only the whistling of the wind about the horse's ears and his own coat collar.

Suddenly a dark patch showed in front of him. His heart began to beat with joy, and he rode on toward the object, already seeing in it the house walls of a village. But the dark patch was not stationary, it moved. It was not a village, but a ridge, covered with tall mugwort, which rose up through the snow, and bent to one side under the force of the wind. The sight of the high grass, tormented by the pitiless wind, somehow made Vasily Andreyevich tremble, and he started to ride away hastily, not perceiving that in approaching the place, he had quite turned out of his first direction, and that now he was heading the opposite way. He was still confident that he rode toward where the forester's hut should be. But the horse seemed always to make toward the right, and Vasily Andreyevich had to guide it toward the left.

Again a dark patch appeared before him; again he rejoiced, believing that now surely he saw a village. But once more it was the ridge, covered with high grass, shaking ominously, and as before, frightening Vasily Andreyevich. But it was not the same ridge of grass, for near it was a horse track, now disappearing in the snow. Vasily Andreyevich stopped, bent down, and looked carefully: a horse track, not yet snow-covered; it could only be the hoofprints of his own horse. He was evidently moving in a small circle. "And I am perishing in this way," he thought. To repress his terror, he urged on the horse still more, peering into the mist of snow, in which he saw nothing but flitting and fitful points of light. Once he thought he heard either the barking of dogs or the howling of wolves, but the sounds were so faint and indistinct that he could not be sure whether he had heard them or imagined them; and he stopped to strain his ears and listen.

Suddenly a terrible, deafening cry beat upon his ears, and everything began to tremble and quake about him. Vasily Andreyevich seized the horse's neck, but that also shook, and the terrible cry rose still more frightfully. For some moments Vasily Andreyevich was beside himself and could not understand what had happened. It was only this: Moukhorta, whether to encourage himself or to call for help, had neighed, loudly and resonantly.

"The devil! How that cursed horse frightened me!" said Vasily Andreyevich to himself. But even when he understood the cause of his terror, he could not shake it off.

"I must bethink myself, steady myself," he went on, even while, unable to regain his self-control, he urged forward the horse without noting that he was now going with the wind instead of against it. His body, especially where his fur coat did not protect it against the pad, was freezing, shivering and aching all over. He forgot all about the forester's hut and desired one thing only—to get back to the sleigh, that he might not perish alone, like that mugwort in the midst of the terrible waste of snow.

Without warning, the horse suddenly stumbled under him, caught in a snowdrift, began to plunge, and fell on his side. Vasily Andreyevich jumped off, dragged down the breeching with his foot, and turned the pad around by holding to it as he jumped. As soon as he was clear, the horse righted itself, plunged forward one leap and then another, and neighing again, with the sacking and breeching trailed after him, disappeared, leaving Vasily Andreyevich alone in the snowdrift. The latter pressed on after the horse, but the snow was so deep, and his fur coat so heavy, that, sinking over the knee at each step, he was out of breath after not more than twenty paces, and stopped. "The forest, the sheep, the farms, the shop, the taverns," thought he, "how can I leave them? What is really the matter? This is impossible!" surged through his head. And he had a strange recollection of the wind-shaken mugwort that he had ridden past twice, and such a terror seized him that he lost all sense of the reality of what was happening. He thought, "Is not this all a dream?"—and tried to wake himself. But there was no awakening. The snow was real, lashing his face and covering him; and it was a real desert in which he was now alone, like that mugwort, waiting for inevitable, speedy, and incomprehensible death.

"Queen in heaven, Nicholas the miracle doer, sustainer of the faithful!"—He recalled yesterday's Te Deums; the shrine with the black image in a golden chasuble; the tapers that he sold for the shrine, and that, as they were at once returned to him, he used to put back in the store chest hardly touched by the flame. And he began to implore that same Nicholas—the miracle doer—to save him, vowing to the saint a Te Deum and tapers. But in some way, here, he clearly and without a doubt realized that the image, chasuble, tapers, priests, thanksgivings, and so forth, while very important and necessary in their place, in the church, were of no service to him now; and that between those tapers and Te Deums, and his own disastrous plight, there could be no possible relation.

"I must not give up; I must follow the horse's tracks, or they, too, will be snowed over." The thought struck him, and he made on. But despite his resolution to walk quietly, he found himself running, falling down every minute, rising and falling again. The hoofprints were already almost indistinguishable where the snow was shallow. "I am lost!" thought Vasily Andreyevich, "I shall lose this track as well!" But at that instant, casting a glance in front, he saw something dark. It was the horse, and not him alone, but the sleigh, the shafts. Moukhorta, with the pad twisted around and the trailed breeching and sacking, was standing, not in his former place, but nearer to the shafts, and was shaking his head, drawn down by the reins beneath his feet. It appeared that Vasily Andreyevich had stuck in the same ravine into which they had, with Nikita, previously plunged, that the horse had led him back to the sleigh, and that he had dismounted at not more than fifty paces from the place where the sleigh lay.

IX

When Vasily Andreyevich, with great difficulty, regained the sleigh, he seized upon it and stood motionless for a long time, trying to calm himself and to take breath. Nikita was not in his old place, but something was lying in the sleigh, something already covered with snow; and Vasily Andreyevich guessed it to be Nikita. His terror had now quite left him; if he felt any fear, it was lest that terror should return upon him in the way he had experienced it when on the horse, and especially when he was alone in the snowdrift. By any and every means, he must keep away that terror; to do that, he must forget himself, think about something else; something must be done. Accordingly, the first thing he did was to turn his back to the wind and throw open his fur cloak. As soon as he felt a little refreshed, he shook out the snow from his boots and gloves, bound up his girdle again, tight and low down, as though making ready for work, as he did when going out to buy grain from the peasants' carts. The first step to take, it appeared to him, was to free the horse's legs. And he did this; then clearing the rein, he tied Moukhorta to the iron cramp in front of the sleigh, as before, and walking around the horse's quarters, he adjusted the pad, breeching, and sacking. But as he did this, he perceived a movement in the sleigh; and Nikita's head rose out of the snow that was about it. With obvious great difficulty, the peasant rose and sat up; and in a strange fashion, as though he were driving away flies, waved his hand before his face, saying something which Vasily Andreyevich interpreted as a call to himself.

Vasily Andreyevich left the sack unadjusted and went to the sleigh.

"What is the matter with you?" he asked. "What are you saying?"

"I am dy-y-ing, that's what's the matter," said Nikita brokenly, struggling for speech. "Give what I have earned to the lad. Or to the wife; it's all the same."

"What, are you really frozen?" asked Vasily Andreyevich.

"I can feel I've got my death. Forgiveness . . . for Christ's sake . . . ," said Nikita in a sobbing voice, continuing to wave his hand before his face, as if driving away flies.

Vasily Andreyevich stood for half a minute quiet and still; then suddenly, with the same resolution with which he used to strike hands over a good bargain, he took a step back, turned up the sleeves of his fur coat, and using both hands, began to rake the snow from off Nikita and the sleigh. That done, Vasily Andreyevich quickly took off his belt, made ready the fur coat, and moving Nikita with a push, he lay down on him, covering him not only with the fur coat, but with the full length of his own body, which glowed with warmth.

Adjusting with his hands the skirts of his coat, so as to come between Nikita and the bark matting of the sleigh, and tucking the tail of the coat between his knees, Vasily Andreyevich lay flat, with his head against the bark matting in the sleigh front. He no longer could hear, either the stirring of the horse or the wind's whistling; he had ears only for the breathing of Nikita. At first, and for a long time, Nikita lay without a sign; then he sighed deeply, and moved, evidently with returning warmth.

"Ah, there you are! And yet you say 'die.' Lie still, get warm, and we shall . . . ," began Vasily Andreyevich. But to his own surprise, he could not speak: because his eyes were filled with tears, and his lower jaw began to quiver strongly. He said no more; only swallowed down the risings in his throat.

"I have been frightened, that is clear, and have lost my nerve," he thought of himself. But this weakness came not as an unpleasant sensation; rather as a notable, and hitherto unknown, delight.

"That's what we are!" he said to himself, with a strange, tender, and tranquil sense of victory. He lay quiet for some time, wiping his eyes with the fur of his coat, and returning the right skirt under his knees as the wind continually turned it up.

He felt a passionate desire to let someone else know of his happy condition.

"Nikita!" he said.

"It's comfortable," came an answer from below.

"So it is, friend! I was nearly lost. And you would have been frozen, and I should . . ."

But here again his face began to quiver, and his eyes once more filled with tears; he could say no more.

"Well, never mind," he thought, "I know well enough myself what I know," and he kept quiet.

Several times he looked at the horse, and saw that his back was uncovered and the sacking and breeching were hanging down nearly to the snow. He ought to get up and cover the horse; but he could not bring himself to leave Nikita for even a moment and so disturb that happy situation in which he felt himself; for he had no fear now.

Nikita warmed him from below, and the fur coat warmed him from above; but his hands, with which he held the coat skirts down on both sides of Nikita, and his feet, from which the wind continually lifted the coat, began to freeze. But he did not think of them. He thought only of how to restore the man who lay beneath him.

"No fear, he will not escape," he said to himself as Nikita grew warmer; and he said this boastingly, in the way he used to speak of his buying and selling.

Then he lay for a long while. At first his thoughts were filled with impressions of the snowstorm, the shafts of the sleigh, the horse under the sleigh bow, all jostling before his eyes; he recollected Nikita, lying under him; then upon these impressions rose others, of the feast, his wife, the commissary of police, the taper box; then again of Nikita, this time lying under the taper box. Then came apparitions of peasants at their trafficking, and white walls, and iron-roofed houses, with Nikita stretched out beneath; then all was confused, one thing running into another, like the colors in the rainbow, which blend into one whiteness, all the different impressions fused into one nothing; and he fell asleep. For a long time he slept dreamlessly; but before daybreak dreams visited him again. He was once more standing beside the taper box, and Tikhon's wife asked him for a five-kopeck taper, for the feast; he wanted to take the taper and give it to her, but he could not move his hands, which hung down, thrust tightly into his pockets. He wanted to walk around the box; but his feet would not move; his goloshes, new and shiny, had grown to the stone floor, and he could neither move them nor take out his feet. All at once the box ceased to be a taper box, and turned into a bed; and Vasily Andreyevich saw himself lying, face downward, on the taper box, which was his own bed at home. Thus lying, he was unable to get up; and yet he must get up, because Ivan Matveich, the commissary of police, would soon call upon him, and with Ivan Matveich he must either bargain for the forest or set the breeching right on Moukhorta. He asked his wife, "Well, has he not come?" "No," she said, "he has not." He heard someone drive up to the front door. It must be he. No, whoever it was, he has gone past. "Mikolayevna, Mikolayevna! What, has he not come yet?" No. And he lay on the bed, still unable to rise, and still waiting, a waiting that was painful, and yet pleasant. All at once, his joy was fulfilled; the expected one came; not Ivan Matveich, the commissary of police, but another; and yet the one for whom he had waited. He came, and called to him; and he that called was he who had bidden him lie down upon Nikita. Vasily Andreyevich was glad because that one had visited him. "I am coming," he cried joyfully. And the cry awoke him.

He wakes, but wakes in quite another state than when he

79

fell asleep. He wants to rise, and cannot; to move his arm, and cannot—his leg, and he cannot do that. He wants to turn his head, and cannot do even so much. He is surprised, but not at all disturbed by this. He divines that this is death, and is not at all disturbed even by that. And he remembers that Nikita is lying under him, and that he has gotten warm and is alive; and it seems to him that he is Nikita, and Nikita is he, that his life is not in himself, but in Nikita. He makes an effort to listen, and hears the breathing, even the slight snoring, of Nikita. "Nikita is alive, and therefore I also am alive!" he says to himself triumphantly. And something quite new, such as he had never known in all his life, is stealing down upon him.

He remembers his money, the shop, the house, the buying and selling, the Mironovs' millions; and he really cannot understand why that man, called Vasily Brekhunov, had troubled with all those things with which he had troubled himself. "Well, he did not know what it was all about," he thinks, concerning this Vasily Brekhunov. "He did not know, but now I know. No mistake this time; *now I know.*" And again he hears the summons of that one who had before called him. "I am coming, I am coming," all his being speaks joyfully and tenderly. And he feels himself free; with nothing to encumber him more. And nothing more, in this world, saw, heard, or felt Vasily.

Around about, all was as before. The same whirling snow, driving upon the fur coat of the dead Vasily Andreyevich, upon Moukhorta, whose whole body shivered, and upon the sleigh now hardly to be seen, with Nikita lying in the bottom of it, kept warm beneath his now dead master.

X

Toward daybreak, Nikita awoke. The cold roused him, again creeping along his back. He had dreamed that he was driving from the mill with a cartload of his master's flour, and that near Liapin's, in turning at the bridge end, he got the cart stuck. And he saw that he went beneath the cart, and lifted it with his back, adjusting his strength to it. But, wonderful!—the cart did not stir, it stuck to his back, so that he could neither lift nor get from under. It crushed his back. And how cold it was! He must get away somehow.

"That's enough," he cried to whoever, or whatever, it was that pressed his back with the cart. "Take the sacks out!" But the cart still pressed him, always colder and colder; and suddenly a peculiar knocking awoke him completely, and he remembered all. The cold cart—that was his dead and frozen master, lying upon him. The knocking was from Moukhorta, who struck twice on the sleigh with his hooves.

"Andreyevich, eh, Andreyevich!" says Nikita inquiringly, straightening his back and already guessing the truth. But Andreyevich does not answer, and his body and legs are hard, and cold, and heavy, like iron weights.

"He must have died. May his be the kingdom of heaven!" thinks Nikita. He turns his head, digs with his hand through the snow about him, and opens his eyes. It is daylight. The wind still whistles through the shafts, and the snow is still falling, but with a difference, not lashing upon the bark matting as before, but silently covering the sleigh and horse, ever deeper and deeper; and the horse's breathing and stirring are no more to be heard. "He must be frozen too," thinks Nikita. And in fact, those hoof strokes upon the sleigh were the last struggles of Moukhorta, by that time quite benumbed, to feel his legs.

"God, Father, it seems thou callest me as well," says Nikita to himself. "Let Thy holy will be done. But it is. . . . Still, one cannot die twice, and must die once. If it would only come quicker! . . ." And he draws in his arm again, shutting his eyes; and he loses consciousness, with the conviction that this time he is really going to die altogether.

About dinnertime on the next day, the peasants with their shovels dug out Vasily Andreyevich and Nikita, only seventy yards from the road, and half a mile from the village. The wind had hidden the sleigh in snow, but the shafts and the handkerchief were still visible. Moukhorta, over his belly in snow, with the breeching and sacking trailing from his back, stood all whitened, his dead head pressed in upon the apple of his throat; his nostrils were fringed with icicles, his eyes filled with rime and frozen around as with tears. In that one night he had become so thin that he was nothing but skin and bone. Vasily Andreyevich was stiffened like a frozen carcass, and he lay with his legs spread apart, just as he was when they rolled him off Nikita. His prominent hawk eyes were shriveled up, and his open mouth under his clipped mustache was filled with snow. But Nikita, though chilled through, was alive. When he was roused, he imagined he was already dead and that the happenings about him were by this time not in this world, but in another. When he heard the shouts of the peasants, who were digging him out and rolling the frozen Vasily Andreyevich from him, he was surprised at first to think that in the other world, also, peasants should be making noise. But when he understood that he was still here, in this world, he was rather sorry than glad, especially when he realized that the toes of both his feet were frozen.

Nikita lay in the hospital for two months. They cut off three toes from him, and the others recovered, so that he was able to work. For twenty years more, he went on living, first as a farm laborer, lately as a watchman. He died at home, just as he wished, only this year; laid under the holy images, with a lighted taper in his hands. Before his death, he asked forgiveness from his old wife, and forgave her for the cooper; he took leave of his son and the grandchildren and went away, truly pleased that, in dying, he released his son and daughter-in-law from the added burden of his keep, and that he himself was, this time really, going out of a life grown wearisome to him, into that other one which with every passing year had grown clearer and more desirable to him. Is he better off, or worse off, there in the place where he awoke after that real death? Is he disappointed? Or has he found things there to be such as he expected? That we shall all of us soon learn.

(*1895*)

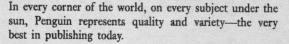